BIRCH

MAPLE

MARITIME
PINE

BAOBAB

DOUGLAS
FIR

PINECONE

EUCALYPTUS

GINKGO

APPLE

MORETON BAY
FIG

GUMNUT

FIG

D1071673

Be a Tree !

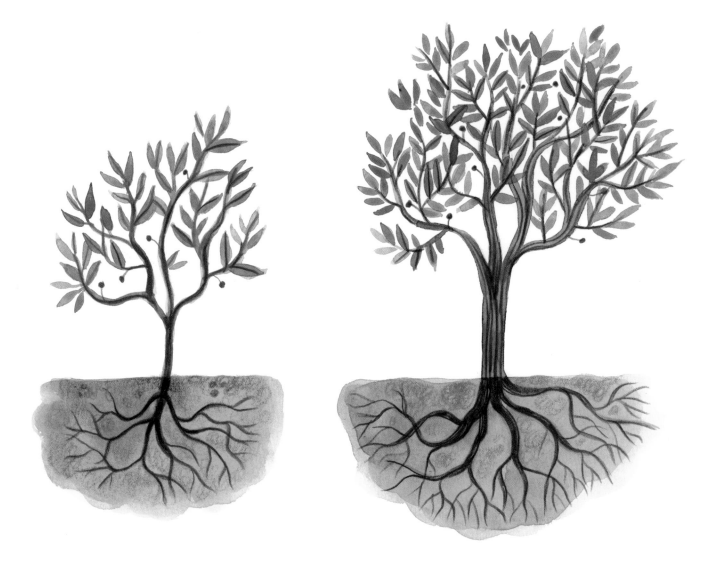

WRITTEN BY MARIA GIANFERRARI

ILLUSTRATED BY FELICITA SALA

Abrams Books for Young Readers
New York

The illustrations in this book were made with watercolor, gouache, and colored pencils.

Special thanks to Geoffrey Parker
at the Smithsonian Environmental Research Center
for sharing his expertise.

Library of Congress Cataloging-in-Publication Data

Names: Gianferrari, Maria, author. | Sala, Felicita, illustrator.
Title: Be a tree! / written by Maria Gianferrari ; illustrated by Felicita Sala. Description:
New York : Abrams Books for Young Readers, 2021. | Includes bibliographical references. |
Audience: Ages 4 to 8. | Summary: Compares the structures and functions of trees to
human bodies, shows the interconnectness and dependence of trees in a forest, and urges
readers to communicate, share, and care for one another. Includes notes on the anatomy
of a tree, ways to help save trees, and how to help in one's community.
Identifiers: LCCN 2020013316 | ISBN 9781419744228 (hardcover)
Subjects: CYAC: Trees—Fiction. | Community life—Fiction.
Classification: LCC PZ7.G339028 Be 2021 | DDC [E]—dc23
LC record available at https://lccn.loc.gov/2020013316

Printed and bound in China
10 9 8 7 6 5 4 3 2 1

Abrams Books for Young Readers are available at special discounts when
purchased in quantity for premiums and promotions as well as fundraising
or educational use. Special editions can also be created to specification.
For details, contact specialsales@abramsbooks.com or the address below.

Abrams® is a registered trademark of Harry N. Abrams, Inc.

ABRAMS The Art of Books
195 Broadway, New York, NY 10007
abramsbooks.com

For all trees.
And in memory of Gracie King, lover of giraffes.

—M. G.

For Nina and Niccolò,
may your roots go deep and your branches reach high.

With love,

—F. S.

Be a tree!

Stand tall.

Stretch your branches to the sun.

Let your roots curl,
coil in the soil to ground you.

Your spine is a trunk,
giving you shape,
holding your crown,
channeling your food.

Your skin is bark:
dead on the outside,
protecting what's within.

Beneath your bark
are layers,
such as sapwood,
carrying nutrients
to help you grow bigger
and taller;

and heartwood,
strong as bone,
to support you.

In your heart's center
is your pith,
keeper of nutrients
when you were a sapling.

High above,
your crown may be round,
weeping
pyramidal
broad.

Let it spread,
shine overhead,
collecting sun
filtering dust
shading your roots on hot days.

Wave your leaves in the wind,
breathe in air,
drink in sun,
let them fuel you
and the world.

See yourself,
branches and leaves above,
roots below,
trunk in-between:
you are a tree.

And now,
look around you—
you are not alone.

You are one of many trees.

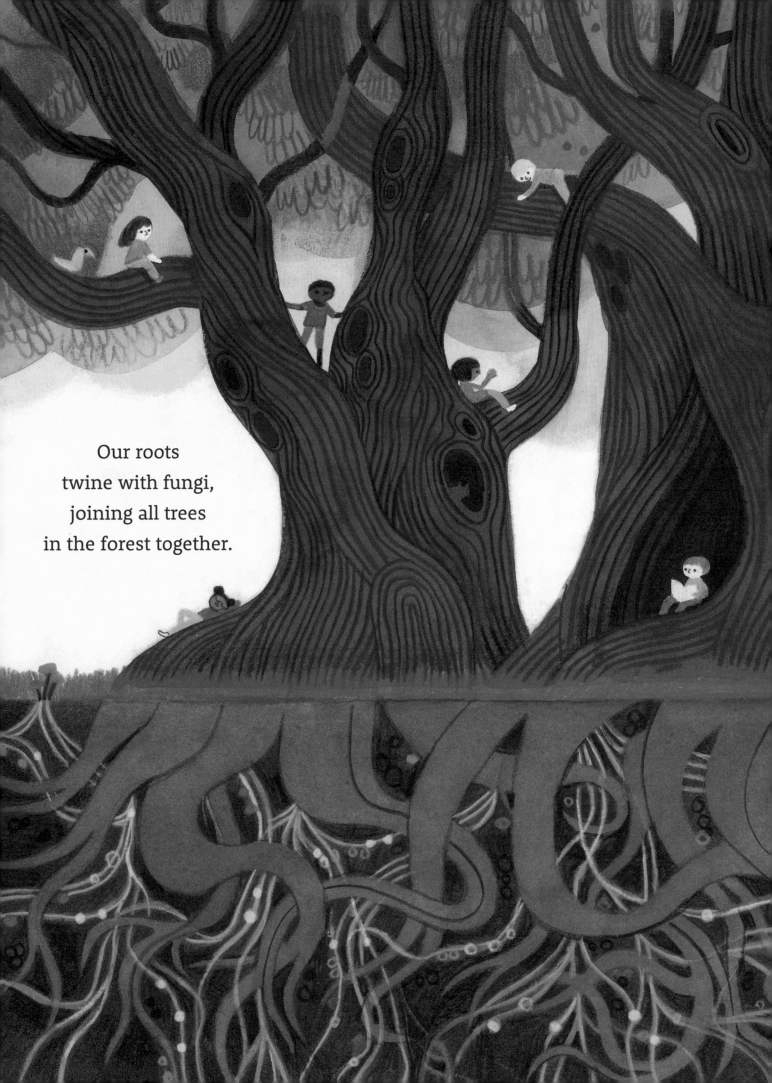

Our roots
twine with fungi,
joining all trees
in the forest together.

We talk,
share food,
store water,
divide resources,
alert each other
to danger.

A wood wide web
of information.

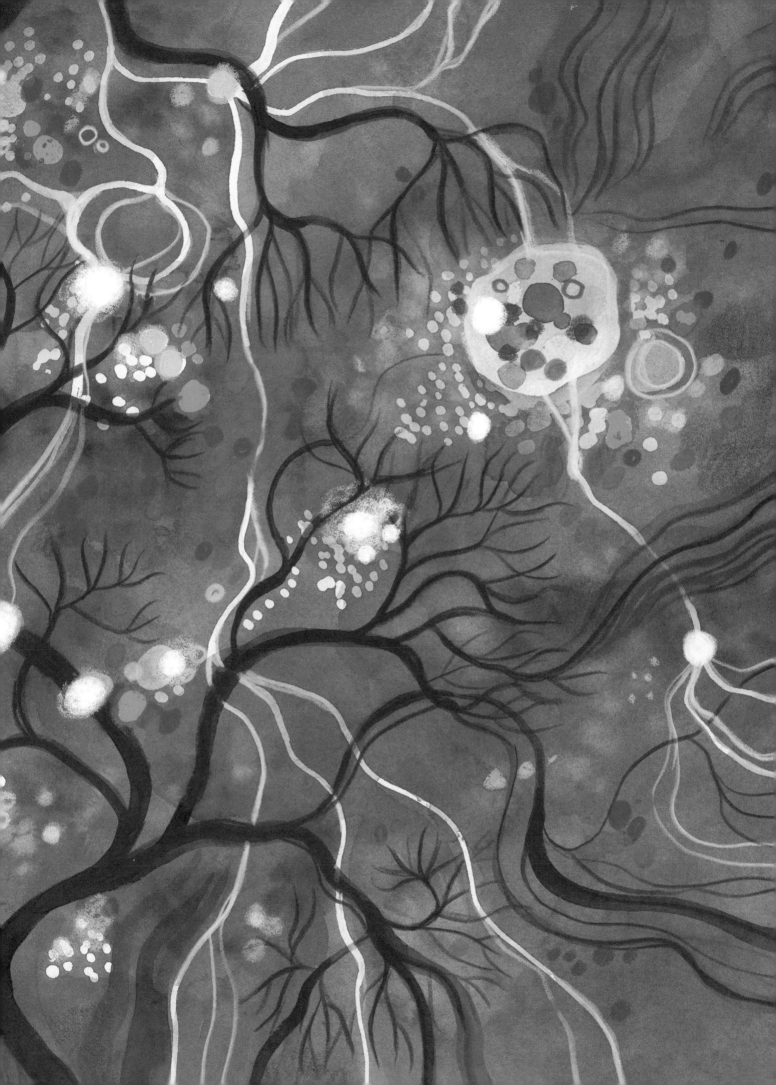

We purify the air.
We anchor the soil,
preventing erosion.

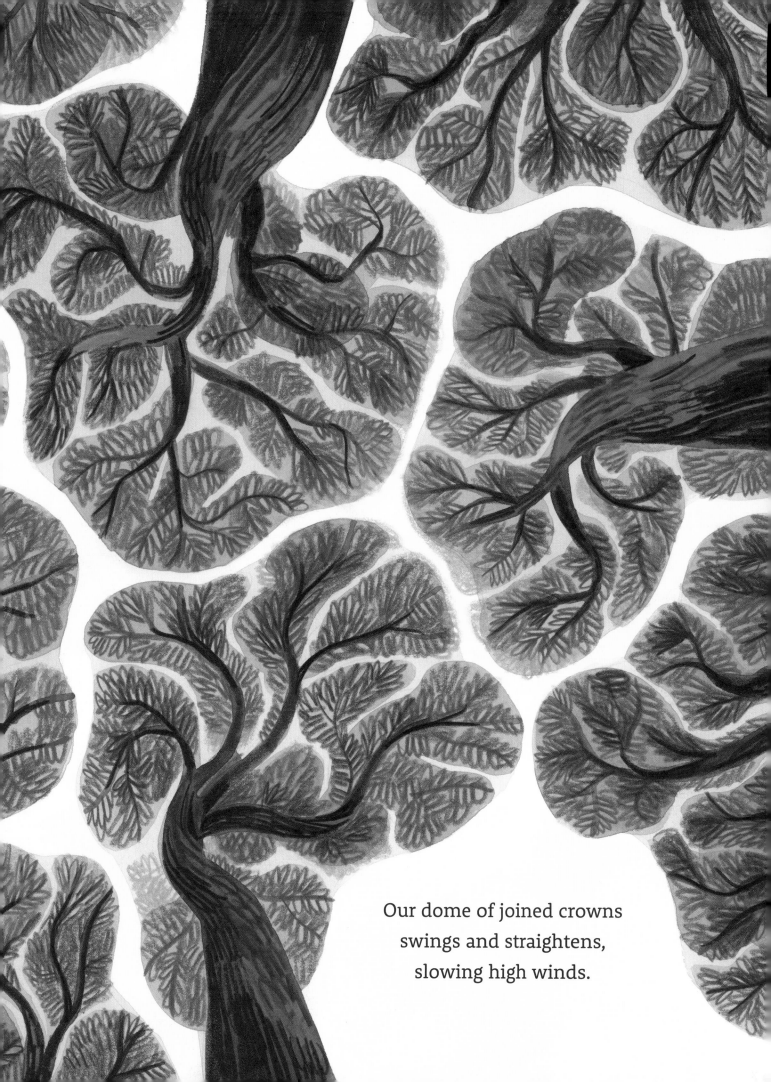

Our dome of joined crowns
swings and straightens,
slowing high winds.

Our bodies and branches and roots are homes
to birds and mammals and insects.

We sustain ecosystems.

But together,
a forest of trees is strong.

Immigrant trees,
away from their native habitats,
are vulnerable.

A family, a community, a country, a cosmos.

Mother trees nurse young trees.
Old trees shade new trees.
Strong trees shelter weak trees.
Healthy trees help sick trees.

There is enough for all.

So, be a tree.
For together,

we are a forest.

Author's Note

Though I've always loved trees, especially climbing them as a young girl, my love and admiration for them has deepened considerably since reading Peter Wohlleben's *The Hidden Life of Trees*. I learned that trees in a forest help protect and care for each other, like family members. Trees with extra sugar share with their neighbors and coordinate their photosynthesis rates so that they can all flourish. There was even a story of how neighboring trees kept a tree stump alive for hundreds of years by sharing sugar!

Trees communicate news—information about insects, droughts, or other dangers—through their intersecting roots, with the help of special fungal networks affectionately called the "wood wide web." Roots and fungi are partners in forest ecosystems, exchanging vital nutrients and learning from their joined neural-like pathways. Immigrant trees, those transplanted and disconnected from their own natural habitat networks, are therefore more vulnerable to damage from insects, droughts, or other threats.

Together, trees help sustain microclimates and ecosystems. They give creatures homes and food—there is nothing better than a shady tree on a hot day. We marvel at their beauty, their ancient elegance. We must do our best to protect them, and we can also learn much as a society from their social system. If we behaved like trees in a forest, by protecting each other and sharing resources of all kinds, the world would be a much better place!

Five Ways You Can Help Save Trees

1. Recycle all paper products, and use fewer by:
   - Choosing cloth towels, napkins, and handkerchiefs instead of paper ones
   - Selecting recycled paper products wherever possible
   - Bringing a lunchbox instead of paper or plastic bags
   - Using cloth shopping bags rather than paper or plastic bags
2. Plant native trees and help preserve mature trees in your community
3. Stage a community cleanup
4. Host a fundraiser like a bake sale and donate the proceeds to an environmental organization. Here are some suggestions:
   - Friends of the Earth International: foei.org
   - The Nature Conservancy: nature.org
   - The Wilderness Society: wilderness.org
   - Sierra Club: sierraclub.org
   - The National Wildlife Federation: nwf.org
5. Celebrate Arbor Day: arborday.org/celebrate

Be a Forest: How You Can Help in Your Community

- Visit with "grandfriends," residents at your local nursing home
- Set up a buddy system with the special needs program at your school
- Make care kits for homeless shelter residents including diapers, combs, toothbrushes, shampoo, razors, books, and other supplies
- Volunteer at your local animal shelter, or read to shelter dogs and cats
- Stage a supply drive for food, treats, toys, towels, and blankets for your local animal shelter
- Send cards to soldiers serving overseas
- Plant native flowers in your garden and neighborhood to attract birds, bees, and butterflies

What other ways can you be like a tree in your community?

Anatomy of a Tree ①

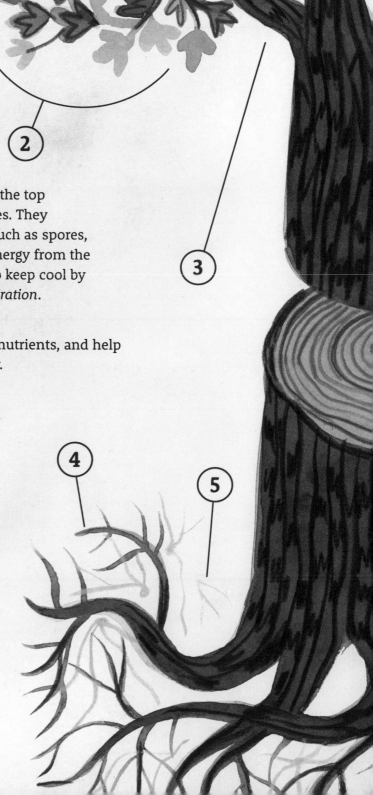

① **Leaves** contain *chlorophyll*, a special pigment that gives them their green color. Through a process known as *photosynthesis*, leaves use energy from the sun to convert carbon dioxide from the atmosphere and water from the soil into sugar and oxygen. The tree either uses the sugar for food or stores it in its roots, trunk, and branches. The oxygen is released back into the atmosphere, where it helps people and creatures breathe.

② **Crowns** consist of the leaves and branches of the top of a tree. They come in different sizes and shapes. They provide shade; they filter dust and other pollutants—such as spores, pollen, even fog and mist—from the air; they collect energy from the sun through photosynthesis; and they allow the tree to keep cool by "sweating" out extra water, a process known as *transpiration*.

③ **Branches** support leaves, channel water and nutrients, and help to store extra sugar, which trees need for energy.

④ **Roots** anchor a tree in place, absorb water and nutrients from the soil, and store sugar. Roots extend through the earth horizontally and can be as wide as a tree is tall. Some trees also have taproots, which descend vertically. Each root has small hairs to enhance its ability to take in water and minerals from the soil.

⑤ **Fungi** are attached to a tree's roots. Together they partner to exchange vital nutrients: the tree shares its carbon with the fungi, and the fungi share minerals from the soil with the tree. Fungi also help trees absorb even more nutrients than they'd be able to on their own.

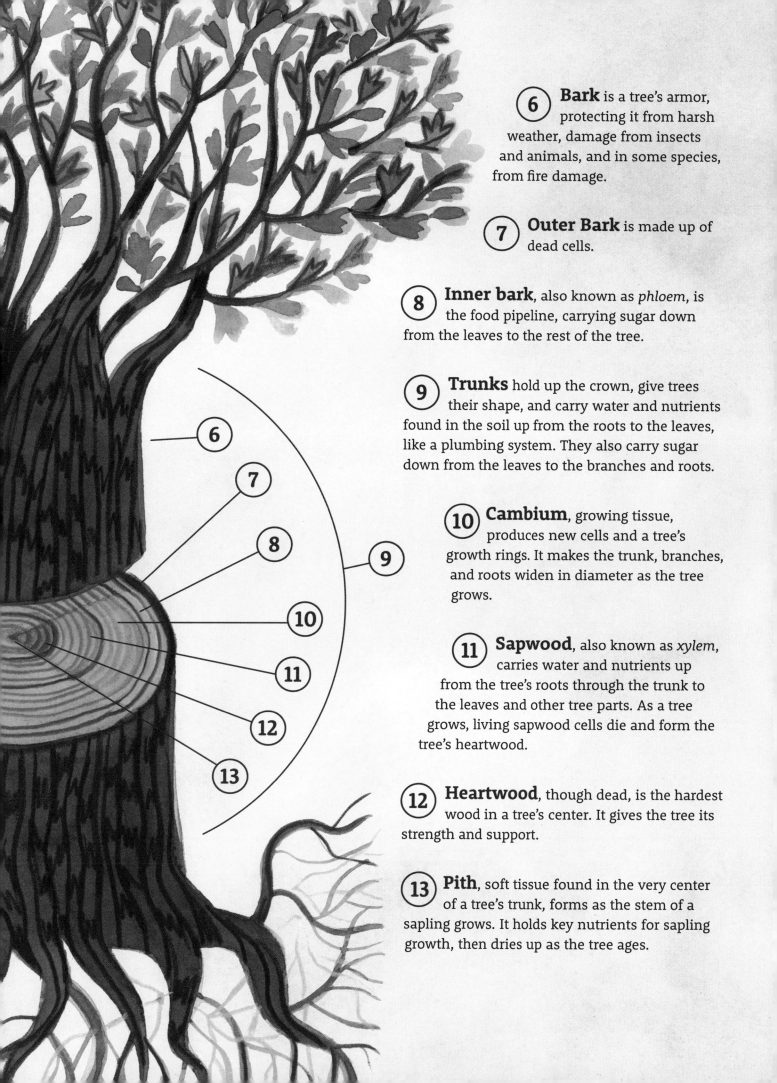

6 **Bark** is a tree's armor, protecting it from harsh weather, damage from insects and animals, and in some species, from fire damage.

7 **Outer Bark** is made up of dead cells.

8 **Inner bark**, also known as *phloem*, is the food pipeline, carrying sugar down from the leaves to the rest of the tree.

9 **Trunks** hold up the crown, give trees their shape, and carry water and nutrients found in the soil up from the roots to the leaves, like a plumbing system. They also carry sugar down from the leaves to the branches and roots.

10 **Cambium**, growing tissue, produces new cells and a tree's growth rings. It makes the trunk, branches, and roots widen in diameter as the tree grows.

11 **Sapwood**, also known as *xylem*, carries water and nutrients up from the tree's roots through the trunk to the leaves and other tree parts. As a tree grows, living sapwood cells die and form the tree's heartwood.

12 **Heartwood**, though dead, is the hardest wood in a tree's center. It gives the tree its strength and support.

13 **Pith**, soft tissue found in the very center of a tree's trunk, forms as the stem of a sapling grows. It holds key nutrients for sapling growth, then dries up as the tree ages.

FURTHER READING AND VIEWING

Hopkins, H. Joseph. *The Tree Lady: The True Story of How One Tree-Loving Woman Changed a City Forever.* San Diego: Beach Lane Books, 2013.

Hutchens, Verlie. *Trees.* San Diego: Beach Lane Books, 2019.

Julivert, Maria Angeles. *Trees.* New York: Enchanted Lion Books, 2007.

Koch, Melissa. *Forest Talk: How Trees Communicate.* Minneapolis: Twenty-First Century Books, 2019.

Sayre, April Pulley. *Trout Are Made of Trees.* Watertown: Charlesbridge, 2008.

Schaefer, Lola, and Adam Schaefer. *Because of an Acorn.* San Francisco: Chronicle Books, 2016.

Simard, Suzanne. "How Trees Talk to Each Other." Filmed June 2016 at TEDSummit, Banff, AB. See ted.com/talks/suzanne_simard_how_trees_talk_to_each_other

Tudge, Colin. *The Tree: A Natural History of What Trees Are, How They Live, and Why They Matter.* New York: Crown Publishing Group, 2006.

Wohlleben, Peter. *Can You Hear the Trees Talking?: Discovering the Hidden Life of the Forest.* Vancouver: Greystone Kids, 2019.

Wohlleben, Peter. *The Hidden Life of Trees: What They Feel, How They Communicate—Discoveries from A Secret World.* Vancouver: Greystone Books, 2016.

WEBSITES

Arbor Day Foundation, "Anatomy of a Tree"
arborday.org/trees/treeguide/anatomy.cfm

"Tree Activities for Kids"
fantasticfunandlearning.com/tree-activities-for-kids.html

National Environmental Education Foundation, "Tree Toolkit: Lessons and Educator Resources for Teaching About Trees"
neefusa.org/nature/land/tree-toolkit

The Teacher's Guide, "Trees/Arbor Day Lesson Plans"
theteachersguide.com/arbordaylessonplans.htm

American Forests, Mission statement
americanforests.org/about-us/mission

Trees For the Future, Mission statement
trees.org/approach

Earth Day Network, The Canopy Project
earthday.org/campaign/the-canopy-project

BIRCH

MAPLE

MARITIME
PINE

BAOBAB

DOUGLAS
FIR

PINECONE

EUCALYPTUS

GINKGO

APPLE

MORETON BAY
FIG

GUMNUT

FIG

OLIVE

ACORN

WHITE OAK

WHITE ASH

HAZEL

WILLOW

WALNUT

BEECH

HORSE CHESTNUT

HOLLY

POPLAR